THE ADVENTURES OF HUCKLEBERRY FINN

MARK TWAIN

Condensed and Adapted by
CLAY STAFFORD

Illustrated by
RUTH PALMER

Dalmatian Press

The Junior Classics have been
adapted and illustrated with care and thought
to introduce you to a world of famous authors, characters, ideas,
and great stories that have been loved for generations.

Editor — Kathryn Knight
Creative Director — Gina Rhodes-Haynes
And the entire classics project team
of Dalmatian Publishing Group

THE ADVENTURES OF HUCKLEBERRY FINN

FOREWORD

A note to the reader—

A classic story rests in your hands. The characters are famous. The tale is timeless.

This Junior Classic edition of *Huckleberry Finn* has been carefully condensed and adapted from the original version (which you really *must* read when you're ready for every detail). We kept the well-known phrases for you. We kept Mark Twain's style. And we kept the important imagery and heart of the tale.

Literature is terrific fun! It encourages you to think. It helps you dream. It is full of heroes and villains, suspense and humor, adventure and wonder, and new ideas. It introduces you to writers who reach out across time to say: "Do you want to hear a story I wrote?"

Curl up and enjoy.

CONTENTS

CHARACTERS

HUCKLEBERRY FINN — a boy who'd rather think for himself (and not be civilized)

TOM SAWYER — Huck Finn's best buddy

WIDOW DOUGLAS — the rich old lady who takes Huck in

MISS WATSON — the widow's sister who wants to civilize Huck

JIM — Miss Watson's slave who runs away to be free

BEN ROGERS, JOE HARPER, TOMMY BARNES — some of Tom and Huck's buddies

JUDGE THATCHER — a good man who keeps Huck's $6,000 safe for him

PAP — Huck's mean ol' dad who wants Huck's $6,000

SARAH MARY WILLIAMS/GEORGE PETERS — a girl… no, a boy… no, Huck Finn in disguise

THE DUKE — the younger of the two "actors" who meet up with Huck and Jim

THE KING — the older of the two "actors" who lie, cheat, and steal

CHARACTERS

MARY JANE, SUSAN AND JOANNA — the three daughters of Peter Wilks, who has died

HARVEY AND WILLIAM WILKS — the English Uncles of the three girls... but not really...

HARVEY AND WILLIAM WILKS — the English Uncles of the three girls... really...

DOCTOR ROBINSON — the only one who sees through the fraud

LEVI BELL — a lawyer with a good idea

UNCLE SILAS PHELPS — Huck's new "Uncle," Tom's real uncle, Jim's captor

AUNT SALLY — Huck's new "Aunt," Tom's real aunt

TOM SAWYER — Huck's new name, Tom's real name

SID SAWYER — Tom's brother, played by Tom himself, because Huck is Tom... Aw, read the book!

NAT — a slave who takes food to a locked-up runaway (Jim!)

NOTICE

This tale has no reason,
No lesson can be found.
If you want a moral,
Quick! Put this story down!

B<small>Y</small> O<small>RDER OF THE</small> A<small>UTHOR</small>

THE ADVENTURES OF
HUCKLEBERRY FINN

CHAPTER ONE

Huck Is Civilized –
Tom's Gang – Fishhooks

Unless you've read *The Adventures of Tom Sawyer* (which I hope you have), you don't know me. That book ended with Tom Sawyer and me finding hidden money in a cave. Because we found it, Judge Thatcher let us keep it. He put it in a bank for us, and we got a dollar a day. By anybody's standards, we were rich.

I've taken care of myself most of my life—though I'm still a kid. I wore what I wanted, slept where I wanted. After I became rich, a woman named Widow Douglas adopted me. She said she was going to "civilize" me. She dressed me up in

fancy clothes that itched and made me sweat. I ran away once, but Tom Sawyer found me and talked me into coming back.

Widow Douglas had rules aplenty. You had to come when she rang a bell, learn about dead people in the Bible, say prayers over food, sit straight, stand straight, and not smoke (even though she dipped snuff). I put up with it until Widow Douglas's sister, Miss Watson, came to live with us. She tried to teach me to read. I told her "no thanks." She told me I'd go to the Bad Place. I told her that would be fine by me. Since she had said earlier that Tom Sawyer would be there, I figured I'd be in good company.

After that lecture, I stole upstairs and sat by the window. (Owls hooted about someone who *had* died. Dogs and whippoorwills told about people *going* to die.) I flipped a spider off me. It dropped in the candle wax and shriveled up before I could get it out. Something bad was about to happen. Miss Watson and Widow Douglas snored down the hall. The clock in the town square struck twelve. I heard a twig snap.

"Me-yow! Me-yow!" came out of the darkness. I smiled.

I called back like a cat, blew out the candle, climbed out the window onto the shed roof, and jumped to the ground. Tom Sawyer waited for me behind a tree.

Miss Watson was very prim and proper, but she still owned a slave. His name was Jim. They didn't let him come in the house so he had to sleep on the porch. (I bet he didn't have to learn to read either.)

Just as Tom and I snuck by Jim, I tripped on a root and made a noise.

"Who's there?" Jim asked as he woke up.

Tom and I dropped to the ground.

Jim came down the steps and stood right beside us. After about five minutes he said, "I'll just sit down here until I hear that noise again. Then I'll catch you." Lord if he didn't sit right between Tom and me and almost hit me in the face with his foot. His sitting didn't last long, though, because soon he started snoring. Tom gave me the signal to follow.

We crept down to the river and met Ben Rogers, Joe Harper, and a few other waiting boys. We unhitched a small flat-bottom boat and, using a pole, piloted it down the river to a rocky bluff. As we climbed ashore, we had no idea where Tom intended to take us.

We finally stopped hiking at a clump of bushes. Tom made us swear to keep everything a secret. We all agreed. Tom ordered Joe Harper to light the candles. We then got down on our hands and knees and crawled into a hole that led into a huge underground cave.

"We're going to be a band of robbers," Tom said. He always said we would be something. This time it was robbers. "Anyone who wants to join Tom Sawyer's Gang must sign his name in blood."

We all agreed heartily.

Tom took out a piece of paper. After we pricked our fingers with a pin and made our marks on Tom's paper, Ben Rogers asked:

"What does this club do, anyway?"

"Robbery," Tom said.

"You mean like stealing cattle or robbing houses?"

"That's not robbery," Tom said. "That's burglary. We're robbers. We rob stagecoaches. We might even ransom somebody."

"What's ransom?"

"Who knows," Tom said. "It's just done."

"Look at Little Tommy Barnes!" Joe Harper exclaimed.

Tommy had fallen asleep. Ben waked him up with a pinch. Tommy started crying.

"That's no way to be a robber," Joe said.

"I don't want to be a robber anymore," Tommy said back. Everybody made fun of him until Tommy said he would tell all of our secrets. Tom gave him five cents to be quiet. Tommy agreed to the silence.

We argued over when we should begin robbing. Some said Sunday, but it seemed rather wicked to begin a life of robbery on the holy day. We finally decided that next week we would get together sometime to determine when we would get together.

Ben Rogers called elections because every club needs officers. We all elected Tom Sawyer as first captain and Joe Harper as second captain.

That's how we began.

When I finally got back to the Widow Douglas's, the sun had just come up. I didn't bother taking off my filthy clothes before I went to sleep.

At breakfast, Miss Watson scolded me because of my clothes. Widow Douglas kept quiet. Because the Widow didn't fuss, I thought I'd try to be nice, but changed my mind when Miss Watson insisted I get in the closet and pray.

"God answers prayers," she said.

It made me glad to hear it. She said I should pray to learn to obey. I prayed for fishhooks, which seemed to me more useful. When none appeared, I told Miss Watson through the closet door that praying didn't seem to work. She called me a fool.

I never did get those fishhooks.

CHAPTER TWO

Boot Prints–Dear Ol' Pap–The Cabin

School started, winter came, and I learned to read a few words and do a little math. On warm nights, I still snuck out and slept in the woods. I liked the old ways, but on cold nights I began to like the new ways, too.

One morning I spilled the salt at breakfast (which is bad luck). Before I could throw a pinch over my shoulder (for good luck), Miss Watson caught me. I left the house walking kind of slow, wondering when bad luck would happen. At the garden gate I saw a man's tracks in an inch of fresh snow. I recognized the boot print. I ran to Judge Thatcher's.

"I guess you've come for some of your money," the Judge said.

"No," I replied. "I don't even want to *own* my money. I want to *give* it to you."

"Give it to me? Oho-o! I see. You mean you want to *sell* me your property?"

"Yes," I said. "Don't ask me why and I won't tell you lies."

Being a judge, Judge Thatcher happily wrote up a paper that, he said, sold my $6,000 to him for $1 to make it legal. It didn't seem like the best deal, but the judge assured me it was the best way to go.

I found Jim. He had a hairball that told people's fortunes. I told Jim I saw my Pap's tracks in the snow even though everybody told me my Pap had died. Jim said something over his hairball and dropped it. It rolled a little. Jim got down on the ground and put his ear against it.

"It won't talk without money," Jim said.

I didn't tell Jim about the dollar I had in my pocket, but gave him a fake quarter instead. Suddenly, Jim heard the hairball speak.

"Your Pap is in town," Jim said. "He's got one good angel sitting on one shoulder and a bad

angel sitting on the other. What he does next depends on which angel he listens to."

I left Jim on the front porch, lit my candle, and went upstairs to my room.

I shut the door. When I turned around, there was my dead Pap—sitting in a chair, very much alive. I gasped.

"Fancy clothes, boy. You think you're pretty sharp, don't you?"

"Maybe I do, maybe I don't."

"Don't get smart with me, boy."

His oily black hair and whiskers dangled. His skin glowed white in the candlelight like a dead man's. His clothes smelled like pig slop and hung in rags.

"I hear you've learned to read and write."

"Yep."

"Well, stop it. Your dead momma never learned to read. I ain't learned to read. You ain't going to. What's this?" He held up a drawing.

"That's a picture the teacher gave me for doing my lessons."

He tore it up. "Ain't no more. I hear you're rich."

"I ain't."

"Judge Thatcher's got your money, I heard."

"I don't have any money. Ask Judge Thatcher."

"I'll do that. How much money you got on you?"

"A dollar. But I'm…"

"Give it to me."

I gave it to him because I knew if I didn't he'd beat me. Pap left—and left me wondering what he'd do next.

Pap tried to get my money, but Judge Thatcher wouldn't give it to him. Pap said he'd take Judge Thatcher to court. He started hanging around Widow Douglas's and he treated me pretty bad when he caught a-hold of me. The Widow told him to leave—so he did, but he stole *me* with him! He put me on a flat-bottom boat, took me three miles up the river, and locked me in a cabin. He had a gun, so I couldn't get away.

Two months passed and then Pap disappeared for three days. I thought he'd been killed or drowned. I worried I'd die locked in

the cabin. I found an old saw blade and used it to try to cut my way out. Before I could finish, I heard Pap coming.

He'd been to get supplies. He said his lawsuit against Judge Thatcher had almost reached the court. His lawyer said when it did Pap would get the money. He also said the Widow Douglas had sued for custody of me, and this time she might win. That meant I'd have to go back to reading.

"I'd like to see the Widow try to get you," he said. "I've got a place up in the woods where no one would ever find you."

That thought scared me more than reading. What if he locked me up somewhere and never came back? I decided that during the night I'd try to escape from him *and* the Widow Douglas! Neither life suited me at the moment.

Pap started drinking while I cooked supper. "A widow's got no right to steal a man's son and try to make the son better than the daddy," he said.

Finally, Pap got so drunk he fell onto the bed. While I waited for him to go to sleep, I accidentally fell asleep myself.

"Get up!" Pap said the next morning.

"Huh?" I asked.

"Did somebody try to break into the cabin?" he asked.

"No." I figured he'd seen where I tried to break out.

Pap looked at me kind of funny. Then his head nodded, letting me know his brain finally caught up. "Go see if there's any fish for breakfast."

It delighted me to leave the cabin. As I walked the riverbank, I saw an empty canoe drifting down the river. I jumped into the river and brought it ashore. Pap would be happy to have it. As I climbed on the bank, though, another thought hit me. *When I ran away, instead of running on foot, I could take the canoe.* I hid it well in the vines.

I met Pap on the path. He whopped me up the side of my head for not checking all the fish lines. I told him I fell in the river and it took some time to get back out. He believed me. We caught five catfish that morning.

After breakfast, Pap said, "I need to go back into town. We need more bacon."

Pap locked me in the cabin and I finished sawing out the hole. Then I fixed the hole back so he would not know what I'd done. I went outside to the front of the cabin, took an ax and chopped down the door. Next I squished some boxbog berries in a cup. They looked just like blood. (Most people can't tell the difference.) I smeared the boxbog "blood" all over the cabin. I wanted Pap to think someone had attacked me.

I had another idea. I took a sack of flour, cut a hole in it, and left a trail of flour from the cabin into the woods. Pap would think a thief killed me and stole the flour—and his hunting gun!

I grabbed the gun, some supplies and food, and hurried back to the canoe to wait for the moon to rise.

Night came. Pap came up the river just as I got ready to go. I hid the canoe back in the vines. When he disappeared towards the cabin, I paddled off from the Missouri shore. I stopped several miles downriver at Jackson's Island.

I thought no one would find me there.

CHAPTER THREE

Finding Jim –
Our Island – The Floating House

I awoke that morning to a BOOM! I saw a ferryboat out on the river that was firing a cannon. I could see Pap, Judge Thatcher, Tom Sawyer, and several others on board. The cannon "boom" was supposed to raise a dead body in the river. They were looking for me!

They shot the cannon again, and straight towards me! I was deaf from the blast, blind from the smoke, and expected my spirit to rise from my body at any minute. They didn't see me.

I built a campfire that night and lived lazily, eating food I had taken from the cabin and adding berries I found in the woods. After about a week, I decided to explore the island. Then I smelled something. I hurried through the brush and before I knew it I came upon an open space where a fresh campfire still smoked. I jumped back into the underbrush and half-crawled back to my canoe. I loaded everything in and hid.

By night, I had gotten mighty hungry. I knew I couldn't start a fire on the island if someone else was living on it as well. So I got in the canoe and paddled over to the Illinois side of the river. I'd just finished a hot meal when I heard horses coming. I put out my fire.

"It's getting late," I heard a man say. "The horses are tired. Let's camp. We'll find him tomorrow."

I paddled back to the island, thinking they were searching for me. I tried to sleep but couldn't, knowing someone might be on the island. In the dark, I got Pap's gun and began slinking through the woods. Just at daybreak, I came to the place where I'd found the fire. Lo and behold!

"Hey, Jim!" I said coming out of the bushes.

Miss Watson's slave jumped to his feet.

"Don't hurt me!" he yelled. "I never done anything bad to dead people!"

I told him, "I'm not dead." He finally believed me after poking me in the stomach. "Make up the campfire," I said. "Let's eat breakfast." It made me so happy not to be lonely anymore.

"What's the use when all you've got is berries?" Jim asked.

"Berries?" I asked.

"That's all I've eaten since I've been on the island, ever since you were killed."

I took Jim back to the canoe and showed him all my supplies.

"I feel like I've died and gone to Heaven," he said.

After breakfast we talked. I told him about how I'd squished the boxbog berries and made it look like my blood. Jim was impressed. He told me, "Tom Sawyer himself couldn't have come up with anything that smart."

I asked Jim what he was doing on the island.

"Better not tell," he said.

"Why?"

"There's reasons. If I told you, you wouldn't tell on me, would you?"

"No," I said.

"I ran off."

I couldn't believe it. I'd been taught it was wrong for a slave to run away. But I had given him my word, just as I would any man, and I wasn't about to go back on him. Jim told me he heard Miss Watson planned to sell him to a man in New Orleans for $800. I couldn't believe it.

"Miss Watson's mean, honey," he said.

"She's been mean to me, too," I said. "At least she didn't make you read."

"I would have liked if she did," he said.

That surprised me, but I quickly forgot about it as Jim told me how he had escaped.

"When they left to look for your body," Jim told me, "I took my chance. With the river high, logs floated by on a regular basis. I took one headed here. That log ride made me a rich man. I hear I'm worth $800." He smiled as he said it.

Our island was only three miles long and a quarter of a mile deep. I wanted to explore an area I'd seen earlier in the middle of the island.

The area was a rocky ridge, thick with bushes and steep faces. Almost to the top, we found a cavern inside the rock about as large as three rooms in a regular house. Jim could stand in it without having to stoop.

"Let's bring our things up here," Jim said.

"I don't want to climb this everyday," I said.

"We could hide here. No one could find us without dogs. And there's signs in the air it's going to rain tonight."

I finally agreed.

We got the supplies from the canoe. By the time we finished, it was dinner time. We cooked at the edge of the cave and had our blankets spread inside. The skies opened up and the rain fell. Darkness came. Thunder and lightning. We watched it from the dry room of our little cavern.

"Jim, I like this better than anywhere. Pass me more cornbread and fish, would you?"

"If you hadn't listened to me, you'd be down there, child," he pointed. "Hungry. Soaking wet."

I also might have been drowned.

The river rose so high that, during the next day, Jim and I paddled around on the island in our canoe! Rabbits, snakes, and anything that had to breathe air hunkered on tree limbs and logs to stay out of the flow.

The island stayed flooded for several days. Only at night did we allow ourselves to go away from the island where someone might see us.

One night, while drifting in the river, we found a plank lumber raft—nine boards worth. We brought it to the island.

Another night a two-story house floated by. Jim thought we should climb aboard. Inside, Jim found a man, dead for several days. Somebody had shot him in the back. I wanted to see the dead man, but Jim wouldn't let me look.

We found all sorts of clothes and things in the house that we might need later. We loaded everything into the canoe.

By the time we started back, we had floated a quarter mile below the island. Daylight came upon us. I told Jim to lie down in the canoe and cover himself, 'cause I didn't want him getting caught as I paddled to the island.

As far as I know, no one saw us.

We found eight dollar coins sewn in some of the dresses we took from the floating house.

"I think these clothes were stolen," Jim said.

"How do you figure?" I asked.

"If someone knew the money was sewn into the hems, would they have left the money behind? Whoever had these clothes last didn't know the money was there."

"They musta killed that man, too," I said.

"It's bad luck to talk about the dead," Jim said.

"Bad luck? If this is bad luck, I'd like more of it." I held up eight dollars.

"Bad luck's coming, child," said Jim.

Days passed and boredom set in. I wanted to go to town. We decided to dress me as a girl using the clothes we'd found in the floating house. A bonnet would hide my face.

When dark came, I paddled to shore. The current drifted me below the town, in front of a little shanty. Through the window, I saw a woman. I didn't know her, so I figured she shouldn't know me. I decided she could tell me the latest news about my death and Jim's disappearance. I knocked on the door.

CHAPTER FOUR

Disguise – The Wreck – Kings and Frenchmen

"Come in here," the woman said. "What's your name?"

"Sarah Williams," I said.

I told her I traveled by foot from Hookerville, seven miles south. "My mother's sick. I'm hoping my Uncle Abner Moore will help us."

"I don't know Mr. Moore. My husband will travel with you when he returns. We've only lived here two weeks. Times are tough."

"Yes, ma'am."

"It would be nice to collect that reward money," she said.

"What money?"

"Don't you know? The town has offered three hundred dollars for a runaway slave, and two hundred dollars for old man Finn. Folks suspect one of them may have murdered that boy. You've heard about the murder?"

"Yes, ma'am," I said. "Awful."

"Some thinks the runaway slave killed that poor Huck Finn. Others think his own father did it."

I couldn't tell her differently. I worried for Jim.

"The reward money should bring both of them in," she said. "Old Man Finn has probably left the country, but the black man may be hiding around here somewhere. I talked with the neighbors next door and asked them if anybody lived on Jackson's Island."

I stiffened up.

"They said 'No.' I didn't tell them I saw smoke from a campfire burning over there yesterday. For three hundred dollars, I thought to myself, it's worth checking out. My husband and another man are going over there tonight. If they find the runaway, we'll split the money, and the black man will be hanged for the murder of Huck Finn."

I started squirming. I had to get to Jim.

"What did you call yourself?" she asked.

I couldn't remember what I had told her. "Mary."

"I thought you came by the name of Sarah."

"I do," I said. "Sarah Mary Williams."

A rat stuck its head out of a hole in the wall. The woman threw a piece of lead at it, but missed it terribly. "Can you throw? You try for the next one." She fetched the lead and dropped it in my lap. I closed my legs to catch it. "Now, what's your *real* name?" she asked.

"Huh?" Another rat stuck his head out. I threw the lead. If it hadn't jerked its head back, that would have been one sick rat.

"Is it Bill? Or Tom?"

To busy myself, I picked up a needle and thread from the table. "I'm not the prettiest girl..." I said, (I tried to thread the needle, but I shook so badly I kept missing.) "...but you shouldn't make fun of me. I must go."

"You tell me who you are. Are you a runaway?"

"Yes, ma'am," I said. "My name's George Peters. My mother and father both died. The law sent me to a farmer who mistreats me. I couldn't take it anymore, so I dressed in his daughter's clothes and ran away. Please don't send me back."

"Certainly not," she said. "When a cow gets up, which end gets up first?"

"The rear."

"A horse?"

"The front," I said.

"What side of a tree does moss grow on?"

"The north."

"If ten cows graze on a hillside, how many face one direction?"

"They all face the same way."

"You *are* a farm boy," she said. "I thought I might catch you in another lie."

"No, ma'am."

"Well, George, you might fool men with this outfit, but not women. When you thread a needle, hold the needle steady and push the thread through. Don't hold the thread steady and then move the needle. When you throw something, throw it from over your head and miss terribly. And when a girl tries to catch something in her lap, she doesn't clap her legs together like she's wearing pants. Remember those things."

I thanked her and hurried back to the island.

I built a fire. Jim and I loaded the canoe, tied it to the raft we'd hid, and slipped quickly from the island in the darkness as quietly as we could.

We saw no one.

- - -

By one o'clock, we had sailed the raft below the island. If a boat came by, we agreed to leave the raft and take the canoe towards shore. We forgot to bring the hunting gun, a fishing line, or anything to eat. I did remember the eight dollars.

When daylight came, we hid on the bank. We cut cottonwood trunks and covered the raft to conceal it. When dark came, Jim made a hut on the raft out of some of the planks to keep us cool in the sun and dry in the rain. We also made an extra steering oar in case we lost the one we had.

We traveled the next four nights and hid during the days. The towns glowed pretty in the night; their lights reflected in twinkles in the slow water. Each night I'd stop at one of the towns and buy fifteen cents worth of meal, bacon, or something else to eat. Mornings before

daylight I'd slip into the fields and "borrow" watermelons, pumpkins, or corn. Pap said it didn't count as stealing as long as you planned on returning what you took. Widow Douglas said stealing equaled stealing no matter what you called it. I'm sure they both had a *little bit* of truth, so we only took a *little bit* of what we saw.

The fifth night we drifted below St. Louis, Missouri. The lightning and thunder played out something awful.

That night we found a wrecked steamboat. On board we found all sorts of things including boots, blankets, clothes, books, a spyglass, three boxes of cigars—all kinds of useful things. We'd never been so rich.

I picked up a book and started reading to Jim. It made me glad to know how to read. We couldn't move around during the day. Reading about kings, dukes, earls and such passed the time.

"I didn't realize so many kings lived and breathed," Jim said.

"Of course." I read to him about Louis the Sixteenth.

"Why do they talk so funny?" asked Jim.

"They don't talk like us," I said. "For example, what would you do if someone came up to you and said '*Potty-yous, Frankie*'?"

"If somebody said that to me, I'd hit him over the head for calling me such."

"He's not calling you anything," I laughed. "He's asking if you speak French."

"Then why doesn't he ask instead of speaking gobbledygook?"

"He is. Listen, do you think a cat speaks like a cow?"

"No," Jim said.

"Then how do you expect a Frenchman to speak like us?"

"A cat isn't a man. A man ought to speak like a man. Not a cow."

I didn't argue any more. Jim had his own way of seeing the world.

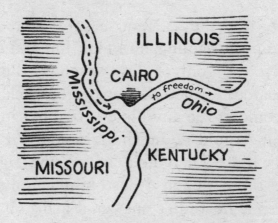

CHAPTER FIVE

In the Fog –
A White Lie – Missing Cairo

In three nights we expected to get to Cairo, Illinois. That's where the Ohio River connects with the Mississippi River. We planned to sell the raft in Cairo and board a steamboat up the Ohio into the free states so Jim didn't have to worry anymore about anybody selling him.

The fog rolled in. We knew we couldn't navigate safely, so I jumped into the canoe and pulled the raft through the fog and swift waters towards an island. The island turned out to be nothing more than a high place with a few saplings. Afraid to go on, I tied the raft to a sapling, but the current became too strong, pulled up the sapling, and took Jim and the raft downriver. In only a few seconds, they both disappeared. I called. Jim answered back. In the fog, I couldn't see anything. I tried to catch him. Sometimes he'd be on the left side. I'd paddle towards him. Then he'd be on the right. I'd paddle there. Then I lost him completely. I called, but he didn't answer. Finally, I let the canoe go where it wanted.

When I awoke, the stars twinkled clearly. At first, I thought I had been dreaming, but then I realized what had happened. I worried for Jim. I saw a black speck in the water ahead. I quickly rowed to it, probably a mile downriver, and saw the raft. And sure enough, there was Jim, asleep. I quietly climbed aboard. The hut had almost collapsed. Twigs and sticks littered the raft. It took several pokes before Jim awoke. He began to cry.

"I thought you'd been drowned, child. I didn't know where you'd gone."

"Drowned? Gone? Have you been drinking whiskey?" I asked.

"When would I drink?"

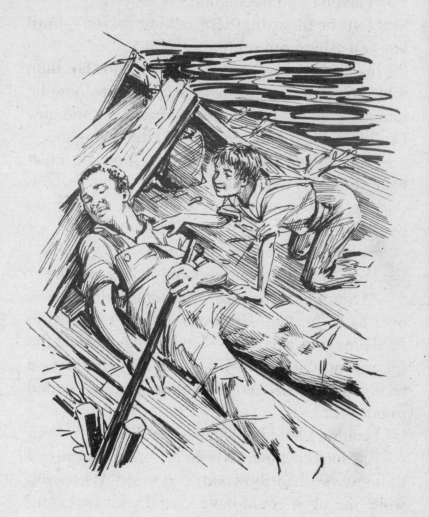

"You're talking so crazy."

"Haven't you been gone?"

"I've been sitting here talking to you—until you fell asleep ten minutes ago."

Jim looked confused. "No," he said. He then told me all about the night according to how he remembered it—how he couldn't find me and how he didn't care if he lived or died after losing me.

"But I never went anywhere, Jim. You must have seen this in a dream."

Jim trusted me more than any person on earth, I think.

"Are you telling me the truth?"

"Yes." I had to fight to keep from laughing.

"Then that's the most frightening dream I've ever had," he said. He then went on to interpret it, telling me what the islands meant, what the fog meant, what the whitewater meant. His face changed. "If I had a dream, then what happened to our hut?"

I couldn't hold it. I laughed until my belly hurt.

Jim looked hurt. "My heart broke because I thought you had drowned," he said. "When you woke me up, I could have kissed your feet. And you want to play me for a fool."

He crawled into what remained of the hut. I tried to get him to come back out, but he wouldn't do it.

After about fifteen minutes, I humbled myself and apologized. I felt so bad I could have kissed his feet.

Jim couldn't wait to get to Cairo because as soon as he got there he'd be a free man. I wanted him to get there, too. Yet, I felt wrong. What had Miss Watson ever done to me, besides trying to teach me to read, that I should treat her this way by helping her slave—her property—escape? But in my mind, Jim didn't seem like property anymore. I felt torn between what I'd been taught and what I felt. I learned two "rights" are not always the same thing. One had to be wrong.

"As soon as I'm free," Jim said, "I'm going to save my money. I'm going to buy my wife from Mr. Blake. Then we'll both work and save. And then we'll buy our two children from Masters Dolan and Crisfield. And if those slave owners don't sell, I'll hire an Abolitionist to steal them."

Such talk put shivers through my spine

because it went against everything I had been taught. I couldn't take it anymore. Surely every white person I knew couldn't be *wrong*. I had to turn Jim in.

"Cairo!" Jim shouted when he saw the lights of a town.

"I'll go ashore," I said.

"You're the best friend I ever had," Jim said. "I've never known a white man to keep his word to me. I'll owe you for my freedom."

Before I could get to shore, two men came by in a skiff.

"Is that your raft up there?" one asked.

"Yes."

"Anybody on it?"

"Yes."

"Black or white?"

I wanted to tell the truth, but I couldn't betray Jim. Something inside me told me *wrong* had to be *right*. "White."

"Five slaves escaped. We've got to capture them before they reach freedom," the other man said. "I think we'll just see for ourselves."

"Please do," I said. "It's my Pap. He's got smallpox. We need help."

"Smallpox!" the first man yelled. "Do you want to infect us?"

"Please, we need help."

"We can't take that chance, boy," the second one said. "Here." The man put a gold piece on a floating slab of wood. "I'll float this twenty dollars to you."

"Add my twenty more," the first man said. "We're afraid to come near even you, son. But we wish you the best."

I cried like I was upset. Then I fished the money from the water. As soon as the men sailed away, I caught up with Jim and showed him the twenty-dollar coins.

I felt good about the money. But I felt awful that I'd lied to those men. And I'd done even *more* wrong—I hadn't turned Jim in. Then I thought how I'd feel if I *had* turned Jim in. I'd feel awful both ways. What's the good of a conscience if you don't feel better after doing one or the other?

Jim saw that I was kinda low. "You be strong, honey. We'll get to Cairo soon enough."

But we didn't get to Cairo. Farther down the river we realized that we were headed down the Mississippi toward Arkansas—farther into slave country. We figured we musta passed the turn up the Ohio River way back in all that fog.

"I should have kept a better watch," I told Jim.

"Don't blame yourself, Huck. You didn't know. We'll figure something out. You just be strong, child. You just be strong."

We made a plan. We would abandon the raft and take the canoe back upriver to Cairo before somebody caught Jim. The sun was rising to the east, so we decided to wait until the next night.

That day we slept. At night, we sneaked to our canoe, but the canoe had disappeared! Because we couldn't make any time pushing the raft upriver against the current, we had no choice but to continue downriver until we could buy a canoe. ("Borrowing" one might send people after us.)

We heard a steamboat. The weather had turned bad, and we lit a lantern so the steamboat wouldn't run us over. Normally, boats traveling upriver stay to the easier shallow water and never get near the swift channel used by vessels going downriver. When fog or bad weather sets in, though, they share the deeper channel, afraid they might run aground in the easier water. That put us both on the same path.

The steamboat came on top of us before we saw her or she saw us.

Bells went off on the steamboat telling the engineer to stop the engines, but before they could stop, the steamboat cut right over our raft. Jim fell overboard on one side and I fell on the other. I dived straight for the bottom to keep from being chopped up by the thirty-foot paddlewheel. I held my breath underwater for

about a minute and a half until my lungs almost burst. When I finally had to shoot up out of the water, the steamboat was tugging up the river, not caring if it had killed us, or what. I called out to Jim, but he never answered. I swam to shore.

I walked about two miles downriver thinking that if Jim had swam to shore, he probably wouldn't trouble himself to swim upstream. Sure enough, there was Jim hiding in a clump of blackberry bushes. I was never so glad to see him! I jumped in the bushes myself. He ran to me and hugged me when he saw me coming. And he had our raft! He said he hadn't heard me calling him because he was too busy swimming downstream trying to catch the raft. We were never both so happy to get back out on the river, in the open—free on the Mississippi.

CHAPTER SIX

A Fallen Duke – A Lost King

For two or three nights, we sailed gently down the river. We relished every minute of it. Nothing matches life on a raft. We watched for candles in passing cabins and used them as our time clock. When they put the last light out in the windows, we knew midnight had come. When the first light appeared again, we knew we had to hide ourselves and the raft.

We found a canoe around the third day. While Jim hid on an island, I took the canoe to the mainland to look for berries to offer a change in our diet. As I paddled up a little creek, two men came running down the bank towards me.

"Save us!" one yelled. "There are dogs after us."

"And men with guns."

"And we didn't do anything!"

They tried to jump into the canoe, but I wouldn't let them. I told them to run up through the brush by the creek, then jump into the water and wade down to the deeper water where I floated. I told them that would throw off the dogs. They did as I told them.

I took them back to the island. Jim helped me fix breakfast.

"So, what got *you* into trouble?" the seventy-year-old man asked the thirty-year-old.

"I sell medicine to take tartar off teeth. Sometimes it takes the enamel off as well. People don't take kindly to it. In the last town I stayed one night longer than I should have. I had to leave in a hurry. That's when I ran into you."

Jim and I looked at each other. The men didn't know one another.

"What about *you*?" asked the younger man.

"I had been preaching a church revival, and making good money at it," the seventy-year-old, bald-headed man said. "I started courting a young lady in the congregation. Unfortunately, her husband found out. A slave woke me up and told me to get out of town quickly."

"Do you think we might work together?" the young one said.

"What do you do?"

"I do several things: Printing, medicine making, theater acting, hypnotizing, fortune telling. I also teach school when somebody lets me. How about you?"

"I'm a doctor by the laying on of hands. I cure cancers and paralysis. I can tell fortunes too if I can hire somebody to check out the facts for me. Mainly, though, I'm a preacher. I save souls."

The young man started crying. Try as we might, we couldn't get him to tell us the problem. Finally, he confessed his true identity.

"I've fallen from grace. It's the secret of my birth. I trust you'll tell no one. By birth, I am a duke. Duke Bridgewater."

I don't know whose eyes got bigger, mine or Jim's. We'd just been reading stories about kings and dukes, and here sat one by our campfire.

"What can we do to get you back to your dukedom?" I asked.

"There is nothing that can be done. Though

it would do me well if you treated me according to my station in life."

"How's that?"

"When you talk to me, call me 'Your Grace' or 'My Lord' or just 'Bridgewater.' Wait on me during meals and do any little thing I want."

We all agreed. By the next day, the old man had turned sour. Finally, *he* started crying.

"I can't go on in this lie," he said. "I must tell who *I* am. The Duke is not the only one thrown from his high place. Can I trust you all?"

We all nodded.

"I am the late disappeared Dauphin, Louis the Seventeen, son of Louis the Sixteen and Mary Antoinette."

"The King of France!" the young man shouted.

Jim and I almost fell over. The King said we could do nothing to help him either, although we could call him 'Your Majesty.' He said when we spoke to him we should bend down on one knee. The King outranked the Duke, so the King expected the Duke to bow as well. We happily waited on them both.

The treatment we gave the King upset the Duke greatly. Finally, the King extended his royal hand.

"We must make peace with each other, my Duke. It's not my fault I'm born a King, nor your fault that you're born a Duke. Let's make the best of this situation in which we find ourselves—plenty of food, an easy life. Let's shake on it."

Before long, I decided we'd found ourselves in the company of two royal liars. I didn't let on to Jim. He fell all over himself waiting on Royalty. If I never learned anything else from Pap, I learned that the best way to get along with his kind of people was to let them have their own way.

CHAPTER SEVEN

Raft Scenes –
A Church Camp Meeting – Acting

The Duke and the King asked us all kinds of questions: Why did we travel only by night? Why did we hide the raft by day? Finally the Duke asked, "Is Jim a runaway slave?"

"Good gracious, no," I said. "Would a runaway slave be running south?"

I told them numerous things about my past, none of which were true. Basically, I "killed everyone off" in my story but me. I said that after everybody died, I had been left with Jim. Because the average boy didn't own a slave, too many people tried to take Jim away from me when we traveled by day. That's why we traveled by night.

The Duke said he would think of a way "to travel by day as people, rather than fugitives."

Ominous clouds formed above us in the night sky. Anticipating a major storm, the King crawled into our raft hut; the Duke followed. Jim had made the hut large enough for only two. Jim and I stood outside as the droplets began to fall. We rode down the river that way the rest of the night. The waves got so strong that at one point I actually fell off the raft. Jim laughed heartily.

The next morning the Duke arose with his carpetbag in hand, from which he produced numerous pieces of paper. One told of "the celebrated Dr. Armand de Montalban of Paris," who could tell people their future.

"That's me," the Duke said, pointing at the picture that looked *nothing* like him.

On another paper he was the "world-famous Shakespearean actor Garrick the Younger, of Drury Lane, London."

On another he proclaimed to be someone else.

And then another.

I almost forgot who he really was.

He pulled out several costumes with frilly sleeves. He told the King that at the next town they would perform scenes from Shakespeare as a duo. "You'll be Juliet."

"How can I be Juliet?" the King asked. "With my bald head and beard?"

"No one will notice. By the way," the Duke said to me, "I've decided how to solve your daylight travel problem. Let's stop at the next town."

When we got to the town, Jim waited with the raft while we went ashore. No one in the town stirred. A slave told us everyone in town was attending a church camp meeting. The King got directions from the slave and said we should join them. The Duke wanted a printing office, which we found. We left him there. I didn't go happily with the King. Everyone always wanted to take me to church, even this scoundrel.

When we got there, we saw almost a thousand people from all over the county. Horses and wagons filled the woods. Lemonade, gingerbread, and watermelon stands were lined up outside. The preaching took place under a huge shed. The preacher held his Bible in the air and told everyone what he held was "the brazen serpent

in the wilderness! Look upon it and live!" He talked the craziest I've ever heard a preacher talk. He screamed. He sweated. He motioned in the air. Pretty soon I couldn't hear him for the noise the people made saying, "Glory!" and "Praise God!" and "Hallelujah!"

The King started praising as well, working his way up towards the front, leaving me behind, and climbing up the stairs. I could hear him yelling over everybody. The preacher told him to speak. The King told everyone he had been a pirate in the Indian Ocean, but after hearing the preacher,

he'd decided to change his ways. He wanted to go back to the Indian Ocean and convert all of those other pirates he knew, but he didn't have any money, but "praise God, somehow God would get him there."

"Take up a collection," someone shouted.

Money started coming forward. Before I knew what had happened, we found ourselves back in the woods running for the raft. The King had collected $87.65 from the crowd. Until he heard the King's figures, the Duke had thought he'd done well in the printing business. He'd sold $9.50 in advertising to people for a newspaper that didn't exist.

While at the office, the Duke had printed a poster. It showed a black man with a bundle over his shoulder. Underneath, he'd printed "$200 reward." The small print told about Jim. Not really about Jim, but a story we all agreed we would follow. We agreed to pretend that Jim had run away from New Orleans and we had captured him to take him back for the reward money. If anyone came along, we would tie Jim in ropes. Jim agreed to the plan.

When it came time for Jim's night watch,

I found Jim trying to get the King to speak French just to see how it sounded. The King refused.

"I've forgotten the language in all this trouble," he said.

Morning came, but, because of the story we'd decided about Jim, we continued to float along. The King practiced his Juliet speech. The Duke made a couple of swords out of strips of wood. He and the King fought with the swords from one end of the raft to the other.

"To make this a truly lively show," the Duke said to the King, "I'll teach you Hamlet's solo speech."

The Duke had to think a moment to remember it—then he began. (I memorized it myself as he taught it to the King because I was so touched by its deepness.)

To be, or not to be—that is the bare bodkin
That makes calamity of so long life.
'Tis a consummation devoutly to be wished.
But soft you, the fair Ophelia:
Open not thy ponderous and marble jaws,
But get thee to a nunnery—go!

At the first town of any size, the Duke had us stop to print small posters that told of the shows. One was for a Shakespeare show, and the other was for something called the Royal Nonesuch (or some such). The Duke and the King entertained Jim and I for the next several days as we floated downriver, looking for a place for our show.

"This is a large enough town," the Duke finally said, somewhere in Arkansas. "Forget Shakespeare. Let's give them something they'll *really* remember."

All over Bricksville, the King and Duke put up notices of the show that read:

AT THE COURT HOUSE!

THREE NIGHTS ONLY!

The World-Famous Tragic Actors
DAVID GARRICK THE YOUNGER!

EDMUND KEAN THE ELDER!
*Of the London
and Continental Theatres,*
In their Thrilling Tragedy of
THE KING'S CAMELEOPARD,
or
THE ROYAL NONESUCH! ! !
Admission 50 cents.

LADIES AND CHILDREN
NOT ADMITTED

"There," said the Duke. "If that last line doesn't bring them in, I don't know Arkansas."

That night, the Duke took tickets from a crowd of men like I'd never seen. He praised the show, lifted the curtain, and said, "I now present to you, here for three nights only, direct from London, the greatest tragedy ever told: The King's Cameleopard."

The King pranced onstage on all fours—all but naked! He'd been painted all over in rings and stripes the same colors as a rainbow.

The audience howled. It was the funniest thing I'd ever seen. The King finished and hurried offstage. The crowd called him back. He did the show again. They laughed even harder. He hurried offstage. The crowd called him back. They couldn't get enough. The Duke lowered the curtain. "Thank you for coming."

"That's it?" one man shouted.

"That's all."

"Royal Nonesuch, I'll say!" yelled one man.

"We've been tricked!" twenty people shouted.

They stormed the stage.

One man yelled, "Gentlemen! Stop! We've been made fools of, our money's taken, but no

one needs to know it. Let's tell everyone what a great show this is. That way, they'll be fools as much as we."

All agreed to the idea.

After the men left, the Duke suggested to the King that it might be a good idea not to do any more shows. For one night's work we made $465.

— — —

When we left Jim, we tied him in ropes. Sometimes we'd leave him for hours. He grew tired of it. The Duke said he'd come up with a different solution.

The next morning the Duke outfitted Jim in a King Lear costume, a white wig and whiskers, and painted Jim's head and hands with blue makeup that made Jim look like he'd been dead for a couple of weeks. He nailed a sign to the raft that said:

Sick Arab – but harmless when not out of his head

The Duke told Jim—if approached—to come out of the hut acting crazy and no one would likely bother him.

With the money we had made, the King bought us fancy clothes. He explained, "There may come a time when we need them."

CHAPTER EIGHT

Getting Information –
The Grand Performance

One morning the King told me to get my fancy clothes on. He and the Duke had dressed in theirs. The King hadn't thought of a plan yet for making more money, but said one would come to him. He needed to check out the lay of the town. To present an image, we needed to arrive in style, so the King had me guide upriver three miles towards a loading steamboat.

Along the way we spotted a young man with traveling bags. The King invited him aboard our canoe, since he was headed for the same steamboat as us. The man at first mistook the

King for someone named Mr. Harvey Wilks, which the King took note of. The King began questioning him about this "Mr. Wilks."

"Mr. Wilks is in passage from England," the young man said, "to see his ill brother, Peter. But I'm sad to say that Mr. Wilks waited too long. Peter died. He left money in a Will to Mr. Wilks. Mr. Wilks will certainly find himself blessed when he arrives. Not to mention the three girls."

"Three girls?" asked the King.

"Yes. They belonged to another brother of Peter and Mr. Wilks. That brother died a year ago and Peter had been taking care of them. Mary Jane's sixteen, Susan's fifteen, and Joanna's fourteen. She's the one who looks odd, but she gives herself to good works. Being a preacher, Mr. Wilks will recognize her good character."

I saw the twinkle in the King's eyes.

"There is another brother, as well," the man said, "who should be coming with Mr. Wilks. His name is William. He is a deaf-mute—and so, of course, cannot hear or speak."

The King went on to questioning the man, all about Peter Wilks's good friends and neighbors, till he about emptied him.

After we dropped off the young man at the steamboat, our "names" changed. The King became Mr. Harvey Wilks. The Duke became the deaf-mute brother, William. I became the servant. Jim minded the raft and carried on like a madman.

We boarded the steamboat and sailed downriver four miles to the town. Some men greeted us. The King told them we had arrived from England. The men offered the bad news of Peter's death. The King cried and wailed. He made all sorts of hand signals in the air, pretending to talk sign language. Suddenly the Duke began crying, but in a silent way. It was the darndest performance I'd ever seen. It made me ashamed of the entire human race.

When we got to the house, the three girls waited on the porch. As they saw who they *thought* were their uncles, they ran to them. Everybody cried. The King and the Duke played it in perfect sorrow, kneeling before the coffin and praying. The Duke, being mute, shed only

tears while the King added words. I've never seen anything so disgusting.

After the King gave a little speech about our journey, the crowd that had gathered began singing. Then the King met with several people in the crowd, going on and on about names and stories he read in letters from his brother who was now dead. (He was just saying the same words we had heard from the young man that we picked up on the river. He had a very good memory.)

Since the brothers had arrived from England, the Will could be read. The dead man gave the house and $3,000 to the girls, and a business, other rental houses, and $3,000 to the two living brothers (the King and the Duke). It also told where the $6,000 in cash had been hidden downstairs in the basement. The King insisted that he, the Duke, and I go down and get it. Instead of bringing it up, the King wanted to count it.

"We want to be up and up and make sure it's all here," he said.

The count revealed we were $415 short.

"We can't go upstairs without the whole $6,000," the King said. "They'll think we stole it.

Empty your pockets and make up the difference. I don't want anyone upstairs to suspect us."

The Duke emptied his pockets, as did the King. They both grumbled about why the dead fool would say there was $6,000 here when there'd only been $5,585. It took most of the money they'd made from the Cameleopard show to bring the balance to $6,000.

"Now we'll take it upstairs," the Duke said, "and count it in front of everybody and give it to the girls in a big show. The crowd will go crazy."

I followed them up.

"Friends," the King said, "our dead brother was a giving man, but we don't need this money. We give it all to these three young ladies, the apples of their Uncle Peter's eyes."

The crowd cheered and cried.

"Hogwash," a booming voice shouted from the back of the crowd.

"Doctor Robinson!" someone called out.

"Ah! You are the good Doctor," the King said to him with his hand out. "My dear brother wrote of you."

"Get your hand away from me. You're telling nothing but lies. You're a fraud! You don't know

Peter Wilks any more than a monkey knows the alphabet. Girls, these men are frauds. I advise you to order them out of your house at once."

Mary Jane, the eldest girl, stepped forward. "Doctor, I cannot believe your tone at our Uncle Peter's death. Our uncles have traveled so far, all the way from England, to be with us. They've done everything to unselfishly prove themselves. They've even given us their inheritance, leaving them with nothing. I know these are my uncles." She smiled at the King and the Duke. They smiled back. It made me sick to see it. "I'm giving them the entire $6,000." She handed over the cash. "Invest this for us. We trust you completely."

"Pig's eyes!"

The doctor stormed from the house.

CHAPTER NINE

Hiding in the Room – Hiding the Money

After the crowd left, Mary Jane gave Uncle William (the Duke) the spare room and gave her own room to Uncle Harvey (the King).

"I'll sleep on a cot in my sisters' room," Mary Jane said.

They put me in the attic.

The girls prepared a large supper. I waited on the Duke and King. The household slaves waited on everyone else. Afterwards, I ate leftovers in the kitchen with the youngest girl, Joanna. She quizzed me about England. I must say I did poorly under the exam.

"I don't believe *anything* you've told me," Joanna said. "You're a liar." She said this as Mary Jane and Susan came into the kitchen.

"Joanna!"

Joanna turned sheepishly towards Mary Jane's voice.

"This young man is our guest," Mary Jane said. "A servant to our uncles. You apologize to him immediately."

"But he said…"

"I don't care what he said. Apologize."

Joanna protested. Mary Jane railed into her. Susan followed. Finally, beaten down, Joanna apologized. What a long-winded and sincere apology it was. I wanted to lie again just to hear it one more time.

I couldn't help but feel badly. Mary Jane and Susan trusted me. Joanna had humbled herself before me. I couldn't let the King and the Duke rob them. I told everyone I wanted to go to bed.

I left them downstairs and then climbed to the attic to think about what I should do. If I confided in Doctor Robinson, he might turn me in along with the two scoundrels. If I told the girls, they might do the same. I decided the only way out of this was to steal the money myself, hide it, leave town with the Duke and King, and then write the girls a note when we had traveled beyond harm's way, telling them where to find the money. I hurried down to the King's room.

I heard the King and the Duke coming up the stairs. I started to hide under the bed, but then decided instead to hide among Mary Jane's dresses. I made a good choice because as soon as they came into the room, the Duke checked under the bed.

"I'm worried about that doctor," the Duke said. "I think we should leave tonight with the money. Let's not be greedy."

"Before we sell off the property?" the King asked. "That's an extra eight or nine thousand dollars."

"We've got more than enough. Why take everything belonging to these poor orphans? Let's leave while it's safe."

"Don't worry for the orphans," the King said. "Once we sell off the property and leave with the money, the buyers of the properties will feel sorry for the girls and return everything to them.

The only ones out will be the buyers. It's the cost of being a fool. Besides, these girls are young—they've got the rest of their lives to work."

I couldn't stand listening to them talk this way.

"I guess you're right," the Duke said. "But I don't like where we've hidden the money."

My ears perked.

"If someone cleans the room, they may find it and keep a bit."

"You're right," the King said. He crossed to where I stood. I thought of what I'd say if he found me. He removed a large box about three feet from my leg. Opening the box, he removed the sack of money. "Let's hide it under the bed. The only way someone would find it there is if they flipped the mattress."

They left. I lifted the mattress and took the sack of money. I carried it upstairs to the attic. I knew better than to hide the money in the house. If it came up missing, the Duke and the King would tear the place apart. I waited for everyone to go to bed. When the house got quiet, I took the money and slipped downstairs.

Everyone slept soundly, including the men downstairs sitting with the corpse. I crossed to the front door. Someone had locked it and I didn't have a key. I heard someone coming down the stairs, so I hurried into the parlor where the corpse lay in a coffin. There was no place to hide the money. Finally, I stuffed the sack under the lid of the coffin. Then I hid behind the door.

Mary Jane came into the room. She prayed over the coffin. When she'd gone and all became quiet, I hurried to the attic.

What an ideal plan! The money would be buried along with the body. After we were down the river, I'd write to Mary Jane. They would dig up the body and get their money back. But then I worried that the man who nailed the lid on the coffin might see the money first. He'd give it back to the King. The King would never let the money out of his sight again. I couldn't go back downstairs. If the men woke up and caught me with the money, the King would let me hang. I didn't sleep at all that night.

The next day everyone gathered for the funeral. Another thought crossed my mind:

What if somebody stole the money off the dead man last night and it wasn't there anymore? When I write to Mary Jane and she digs up the body, maybe all she'll find is a dead man. I didn't dare look to see if the dead man still had the money stuffed between his legs, but it sure was on my mind.

The preacher spoke. Someone played a rented organ. The crowd of mourners sang. The King gave a long speech. Everyone cried. I never heard so much nose-blowing in all my life. When it came time to seal the coffin, I held my breath. The lid went on. The nails went in. They buried the body.

After hugging everybody, the King said he had an announcement. "I'm taking the girls with me back to England. What better place to be than with one's family?"

Everyone, including the girls, was thrilled at the idea.

"We must, of course, sell all the property, including the houses and the slaves," he added.

The next day slave traders bought two boy slaves and shipped them to Memphis. The traders sent the boys' mother to New Orleans. I thought about Jim and how he missed his family. It was terrible to break up a family this way. Some of the townspeople thought it cruel as well, including the Duke. He told the King so afterwards.

"They'll be back," the King said, "when everyone realizes what we've done." I didn't believe the King. It seemed to me that the mother and her children had been broken up for good.

The next day the house was to be sold at auction. I awoke that morning to the King shaking me.

"Have you been in my room?" he asked.

"No."

"Have you seen anyone in my room?"

"Just the slaves."

"The ones we sold?"

"Yes."

The King's face turned so red he looked like a pickled beet.

"Confound it."

"What?" I asked, playing innocent.

"You never mind."

The Duke started arguing with the King. The King fussed at the Duke. I thought they were going to fight right there. They disappeared down the stairs and left me alone in the attic.

CHAPTER TEN

Revealing the Fraud–Another Plan

As I passed the sisters' bedroom the next morning, I heard Mary Jane crying. She told me she felt sorry for the slave family that had been separated. "Mother and two children will never see each other again," she sobbed.

I couldn't take it. "They will," I said before I could catch myself. "They'll be back together in two weeks. If we act quickly."

She hugged me. "How do you know?"

I couldn't think of anything fast enough so I tried something I'd never done before: I told the truth. "It takes several days for money to change hands to make sales final. Mary Jane, is there anywhere you could go for the afternoon?"

"Yes. Mr. Lothrop's. Why?"

"If I tell you how the slaves will come back together, and prove to you how I know, will you go to Lothrop's?"

She nodded.

"Do you mind if I shut the door?"

She agreed.

"When I tell you this, you've got to be quiet."

She nodded.

"Those uncles of yours are frauds."

She waited to hear me out. I told her everything (except for *one* part that concerned a certain coffin...).

She jumped from the bed and cried, "We'll have those men tarred and feathered, right this minute."

"Please don't," I begged. "If you did, I'd be fine. But there's *another* person that would be hurt terribly if you didn't wait." I thought about Jim when I said this. If the Duke and the King knew I had betrayed them, they'd sell Jim back into slavery in a minute. "How far is it to Mr. Lothrop's?"

"Four miles."

"Go visit him and come back tonight. If you get here before eleven o'clock, put a candle in the window. If I'm not back here by eleven, it means I'm safe and gone. When you know I'm gone, tell the neighbors and have these two jailed. If something happens and I don't get away, though, I hope you'll stand by me."

"Of course I will."

"If I get away, I won't be here to prove these men aren't your uncles." I took some paper off Susan's desk and wrote:

Royal Nonesuch, Cameleopard, Bricksville

I handed her the paper. "You contact the town of Bricksville, show them this paper, and you'll have an entire town down here to tell you who these actors are. Let the auction go on today as planned. No money will change hands for a couple of days so nobody will be hurt."

"I'll do just as you say," she said. "I'll go down to breakfast and then straight to Mr. Lothrop's."

"No. You can't go to breakfast. You have to go now. Those trained crooks will look right in your face and know I told you. They'll slide away quicker than a snake. You leave now. I'll make up

something about why you're gone. I'll tell your sisters. There's one more thing. The money."

"I know," she said. "They've got it. We'll just have to get it back."

"*They* don't have it."

"Who *does*?"

I couldn't tell her because I knew she'd never make it out of the house without squealing. I got another piece of paper and wrote down the truth. It took me a while because I write slowly and I wrote the entire story of how I hid the money between her dead uncle's legs. I folded up the paper and gave it to her.

"I'm giving you this to read on your way to Lothrop's. Please don't think poorly of me. I did the best I could considering the circumstances."

"Good-bye," she said. "I'll do everything just as you've told me. I'll think of you often. And I'll pray for you."

Pray for me? I thought, *If she knew me she'd probably want to pray for something a little easier*, but I kept quiet.

I found the sisters sitting around the breakfast table. The uncles were still upstairs, but I had to talk quickly.

"Mary Jane had to leave," I said. "Someone has taken ill at—at the neighbor's house."

"I hope it's not Hannah!"

"Yes, it is," I said. "They stayed up with her all night last night. She may not make it. She has the mumps."

"People don't die from the mumps," Joanna said.

"It's got other things mixed in," I said. "Measles, whooping cough, consumption, yellow jaundice, brain fever. It's a bad mix. Highly catching. Few have ever seen it, not even the doctor. Mary Jane said not to tell your uncles. If your uncles knew she'd visited Hannah on her catchy deathbed, they might postpone the trip to England."

"They *can't* know," Susan agreed. "We can't miss England just to wait around to see if Mary Jane comes down with... whatever it is. And I've already packed my bags."

"Exactly," I answered. "Mary Jane said for you to tell the uncles that she'd gone to tell some people to come to the auction."

The sisters did as I instructed them. The uncles didn't seem to care where Mary Jane was.

Later that day, everything sold at the auction. The uncles smiled until a crowd of folks came up yelling and laughing. Someone called out:

"Here are the *other* brothers of old Peter Wilks! Which set do you think is *real*?"

CHAPTER ELEVEN

The Real Uncles – Digging Up the Truth

The crowd brought a nice-looking older gentleman and a nice-looking younger gentleman over to see the King and the Duke. The younger man had his right arm in a sling.

I felt myself wilting, but the smiling King reached out his hand, as he would greet anybody. The older gentleman didn't take it.

"My name is Harvey Wilks," the older gentleman said. "I'm the brother of Peter Wilks, deceased. This is our other brother, William. He can't hear or speak, and with his hand broken it is impossible for him to communicate. Our baggage unfortunately left the boat in the town before this one, but when it comes we will prove we are truly the proper relatives."

He sounded English to me by the way he pronounced words.

"When did *you* come to town?" a man asked the King. I'd never seen this man before.

"About an hour before sundown the day before the funeral."

"How'd you come?"

"On the *Susan Powell*," the King said. "From Cincinnati."

"Then how come I saw you up at the Point that same morning? You were in a canoe. And you had a boy with you."

They started arguing.

"Would you know the boy again if you saw him?" Doctor Robinson asked.

"Probably not. Why, yes! There he is." He pointed at me.

"Neighbors," the doctor said, "I've told you before these men are frauds. Let's go down to the hotel with both sets of uncles and have this out."

It was almost sundown when the doctor began. He pointed at the King and the Duke.

"If these two men are *frauds*, they may have help waiting to get the money out of town. If these men are for *real*, I'm sure they won't mind if we guard their money for them. Would you?"

"Gentlemen," the King began, "the slaves we sold have *stolen* our money out of our bedroom. You won't find it at the house." The King looked sincere because he thought himself to be telling the truth.

By the crowd's reaction, I could tell we lost support.

The doctor turned to me and asked, "Are you English as well?"

"Yes."

They started asking me all sorts of quizzes about England, which I tried to answer.

"That's enough," the doctor said. "You're not a very good liar, young man."

I was happy he stopped asking me questions, but I didn't take kindly to his compliment.

"I know how to solve this," Harvey Wilks proclaimed. "My brother had a tattoo on his chest. Surely the undertaker can confirm this."

"Wait," said the lawyer, Mr. Levi Bell. He pointed at the King. "What was the tattoo?"

"A blue arrow."

"Wrong!" shouted Harvey Wilks. "It was his initials, PBW."

"There was no tattoo at all," the grave undertaker said.

The crowd gasped.

"Enough!" Levi shouted over the yelling crowd. "We'll dig up the corpse and see."

They dragged us to the graveyard. Thunder and lightning began. Rain fell in buckets. I wished I had Jim close by to tell me if these things were a good sign, or bad. I had my own idea.

Finally, they brought the coffin up and opened the lid.

"The money!" a man shouted. He held up a bag.

The man holding me loosened his grip to get a better look. I made a beeline through the crowd and down the vacant street. As I ran by the Wilks's house, I saw a candle in the window. I wanted to stop, but I ran on. I would have liked to have said good-bye to Mary Jane.

When I reached the river, I borrowed a canoe someone had forgotten to tie down and rowed madly to the raft.

"Jim!" I shouted as I climbed aboard.

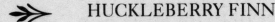

Suddenly, something dead-for-weeks came out of the hut, calling, "Huck! Huck!"

I screamed and fell back into the water before I remembered Jim's makeup. Jim wanted to hug me.

"Save it for breakfast," I said, scrambling. "Let's get out of here!"

When the lightning struck again, I received a horror of a different kind—*the Duke and the King had followed us on a raft of their own!*

CHAPTER TWELVE

Royal Pains –
Jim Is Stolen – Huck's Decision

The King grabbed me. "Tired of being with us? Tell me what you had in mind."

I had to think quickly before the King shook my head off. "The man holding me felt sorry for me. When everyone shifted to look at the money, he told me to run. He said I couldn't help either of you. I hated leaving you behind. Jim did, too."

"That's right," Jim said.

"I didn't address you," the King said. "I should drown you in the river."

"Let go of that boy," the Duke said. "Did *you* ask about him—or me—when *you* hightailed for the river?"

The King let me loose. "That blamed town."

"You should better blame *yourself*," the Duke said, glaring at the King. "A clever trick—hiding the money in a casket!"

"Me?" the King asked angrily. "What about *you*?"

"I have to give you that," the Duke said. "But when you ditched the boy and me, you were going to sneak back to the town, dig up the body, and keep the stash yourself. I should drown *you* in the river!"

"*You're* the scoundrel with the plan!"

The King lunged at the Duke. They fought all over the raft. One choked one, the other choked the other. Jim and I did our own dance to keep from getting knocked into the water.

"Admit it!" the Duke yelled.

"I admit it," the King said as the Duke squeezed the King's neck so hard the King's head turned blue.

Later, they huddled in the hut, each forgiven, sleeping soundly.

I told Jim the whole story.

The Duke and the King tried several frauds in different villages along the way. They started a dancing school, but when the townsfolk saw they danced like kangaroos, they waltzed them out of town. They tried so many schemes, I can't remember them all: playing as missionaries, hypnotizing, lecturing, teaching, doctoring, fortune telling. They spent every cent they had. We hated being with them.

They began talking quietly just to each other, making Jim and me nervous. Then, when we came upon a little town named Pikesville, the King told us to stay put while he went to shore. At noon we were to find him.

Noon came and the Duke and I found the King in a saloon. A bunch of men were arguing with the King, and the Duke jumped into the fight. I took the chance and *ran*.

When I'd rowed the canoe back to the raft, I yelled, "Let's go, Jim! Let's get out of here! We're rid of them. Jim! Jim?"

I couldn't find Jim!

Halfway back to town, I asked a boy if he'd seen a black man matching Jim's description.

"You mean the dangerous runaway slave?

He's chained down at Silas Phelps's," the boy said.
"A man..." (he went on to describe the King)
"...found him first, but sold him for $40 to ol' man
Burton rather than waiting to collect the full $200
reward. Then Burton sold him to Phelps. I saw the
slave's picture on a New Orleans wanted poster."

I thought of the poster the Duke had printed.

I stumbled back to the raft. Jim would be
a much better slave at *home* than down South.

But if I wrote to Miss Watson and told her where Jim was… why, for the rest of my life I'd be known as a blasted Abolitionist. I'd be known as somebody who helped a black slave try to get his freedom. And for the rest of Jim's life, he'd be treated as a slave who'd tried to escape, living a life lower than a stray dog's. The law said Jim was a slave. All the respectable people I knew would say I was doing wrong by helping him escape. So, I *had* to turn Jim back to Miss Watson, his rightful owner. If I didn't, I would be sinning and I could end up burning in the "Bad Place." That scared me. I took out a piece of paper and wrote:

> *Miss Watson, your runaway slave Jim is down here two miles below Pikesville, and Mr. Phelps has got him and he will give him up for the reward if you send.*
>
> HUCK FINN

I felt good. I felt washed of my sins. I prayed and believed God heard. And then I thought of Jim. I thought of days and nights together. I thought of conversations, songs, laughs. I thought how he'd let *me* sleep, instead of getting sleep himself. I remembered how glad he was to see me, if I'd been gone five minutes or five days. I remembered how he called me "honey" and "child." I remembered he said I was his best friend ever...

"I'd rather burn in the Bad Place!"

I grabbed that paper and tore it up.

"Jim will be a free man, whatever cost I have to pay to see it done."

I put on my suit the King had bought me. I rowed the canoe to shore, filled it with rocks, and sunk it, so no one would find it until I came back.

I saw the Duke as I sneaked back through town. While I watched, he tacked a poster on a tree for another "Cameleopard" show. *The Royal Nonesuch was at it again*, I thought.

Whatever the future held for me, I had only one place to find: Silas Phelps's where Jim was held. No matter what it took—risking my own life even—Jim would be a free man.

CHAPTER THIRTEEN

My New "Aunt Sally"– Tom Foolery

When I got to Silas Phelps's farm, it looked like Sunday. Everything was quiet, except for the breeze and bugs.

"Might as well get on with this," I mumbled.

I climbed over the fence and started towards the back of the kitchen. When I got about halfway, a hound growled behind me. More hounds came from the corners. Before I knew it, there were fifteen around me in a circle.

"You dogs get," a black woman said as she came from the kitchen. She swung a rolling pin in her hand. Those dogs lost themselves in a minute.

Three little black children ran behind the woman and, when she stopped, they grabbed her dress and looked around. A white woman appeared at the door. She had three little white children and they acted just like the black ones. The white woman burst into tears and ran towards me.

"It's you!"

"Yes'm," I said as she hugged me.

"Children, it's your cousin Tom! We've been expecting you for a couple of days. Did your boat run aground?"

"Yes'm."

"Don't say 'yes'm.' " She ruffled my hair. "Say 'Aunt Sally.' "

OK, I now have an Aunt Sally, I thought.

"You must have seen your uncle on the way here," she said. "He's gone to town to fetch you. We've gone every day for the past week."

"I got here early so I took my time coming the back way. That's how I must have missed him."

"But where's your luggage?"

"I hid it."

"It'll be stolen."

"Not where I hid it." What I really wanted to do was to get my "cousins" outside and pump

them for information.

"I've been running on and on," Aunt Sally said. "I'll stop talking. Tell me about Sis and the family."

I knew I was up a tree and hanging on the last limb. Just when I thought I'd have to try truth for the second time in my life, I heard a horse *clop-clop-clop* down the road. The woman grabbed me and hid me behind the bed.

"Here comes Silas. We'll play a joke on him. Children, don't you say a word."

I prayed Silas didn't find Tom down at the dock, otherwise there'd be two of us.

"Did you find him?" Aunt Sally asked Silas when he walked in.

"No. I'm beginning to worry."

"What could have happened to him?"

"That's just it."

"Why, Silas! Look yonder."

He looked out the window. Sally hurriedly pulled me up. He turned around.

"Who's *that*?"

"Who do you think it is?" she asked.

I prayed he recognized me as well as Aunt Sally had.

"I don't know," he said. "Who is it?"

"It's Tom Sawyer."

I almost passed out from joy. They thought I was my old buddy Tom. I gladly told them all about everyone back home and the riverboat ride down. They never suspected me, but my confidence shook when I heard the steamboat whistle. What if Tom were aboard that boat?

"I better get my luggage," I told them.

"Silas will go with you."

"No," I said. "I wouldn't trouble you, if I could drive the wagon myself."

I started up the road. In about a mile, I saw a wagon. Sure enough, Tom Sawyer rode as passenger. I'd never seen him so dressed up. I hailed it down.

Tom's mouth dropped. His eyes grew wide. "I've never done you any harm, Huck Finn. Why are you back, you ghost?"

"I'm not back. I never left."

When he heard my voice he eased up. "You're not dead?"

"No. Feel me."

He got out of the wagon, reached up, and touched me. "Huck!"

He had his driver wait while we drove in my wagon up the road a little and talked. I told him my situation, except for the part about Jim.

"You be me," Tom insisted. "Take my trunk for your luggage. I'll show up later."

"What will you say?"

"Leave that to me," Tom said. I did. With Tom and tricks, a body didn't have to have any worries.

"There's one more thing, Tom. I'm stealing a slave. Miss Watson's Jim…"

"What!"

"I know it's wrong," I said. "I've got to anyway. I'm going to set him free."

Tom grinned. "I'll help you steal him!"

About half an hour after I got back, Tom's wagon stopped in front of the house.

"Silas, there's a stranger outside."

The wagon disappeared back down the road. Tom climbed the fence and walked to the front porch like he owned the place.

"Mr. Archibald Nichols, I presume," Tom said with a tip of his hat.

"I'm sorry, son," Silas said. "Your driver dropped you three miles short. Come in, have supper with us, and I'll take you on."

While we ate, Tom talked about how his name was William Thompson from Hicksville, Ohio. I never heard such hogwash. He could run on more than a mountain spring.

Then, right in the middle of a sentence, Tom got up and kissed Aunt Sally on the mouth! Sally jumped up from her chair, wiping and spitting.

"How dare you!"

"I'm sorry, ma'am," Tom said. "They told me you'd like it."

"What do you take me for?" She picked up a spinning stick. I thought any minute she'd crack him over the head.

"Everybody said…"

"Who's everybody?" Sally asked. "You had better say their names or this world's going to be one idiot short."

Tom turned to Silas. "Didn't you think she'd like it?"

"No. I believe not."

"Tom," (Tom looked at me.) "didn't *you* think Aunt Sally would open her arms and say, 'Sid Sawyer'?"

"My land," Sally screamed as she grabbed him. "You rascal."

Tom Sawyer played like he was his own brother while I played like I was Tom.

"I didn't know you were coming, too, Sid," I said to Tom.

We didn't ask about Jim the whole meal, but somehow the topic worked itself around. One of Sally's boys asked, "Can Tom and Sid go with us to see the show?"

"No one's going to the show," Silas said. "That runaway slave told Burton that the people producing it were scandalous. The town's going to tar and feather them if what the slave says is true."

Tom and I were supposed to share a bedroom. We asked to go to bed early. We went upstairs, slid down the lightning rod, and hurried to town. Until we could find where Silas had hidden Jim, I wanted to warn the King and the Duke—so when *their* plans got messed up they wouldn't mess up *mine*.

I saw the townspeople pulling the King and the Duke up Main Street. A man told me the audience had waited for the King to get his clothes off before the town jumped them. Both scoundrels had been tarred, feathered, tied to logs, and dragged about town. They looked like two overgrown chickens on a stick.

Human beings can be awful cruel to one another.

CHAPTER FOURTEEN

Jim Is Found –
Tom's Escape Plot

On the way home, Tom stopped me on the road.

"I've figured out where Jim is."

"Where?" I asked. We'd seen no sign of him.

"Do you remember when that slave took that dog slop down to the hut with the lean-to? By the ash hopper? Did you notice that piece of fruit?"

"Dogs don't eat fruit," I said.

"And the slave unlocked the door? Afterwards, he gave Uncle Silas the key."

"I saw that."

"Fruit? A locked door? That means somebody's kept prisoner in there."

"It's got to be Jim," I said.

"This is how we're going to get him out," Tom said. I would explain Tom's plan in detail, but like most of Tom's plans, it would change itself completely before it got to the end.

"And don't bring up more reasons why I shouldn't help you set Jim free," Tom ordered firmly. "You've gone on and on about my family, about people back home, about what they'd think of me if I go through with this. I know people would say it's not respectable, but I gave you my word, didn't I? Beyond that, I've got my own reasons. Don't you think I've thought about all those things? If I keep my word, that's respectable enough for you, isn't it?"

I still didn't understand why he'd agreed to help me. He had to know what we were about to do was wrong.

The next morning, Tom and I went down to the slave cabins to pet the dogs and make friends with Nat, the slave that fed Jim—if it *was* Jim that was being fed. As the slave loaded up a plate with food, we asked him why he tied his hair up with little ringlets of string.

"To keep the witches away," Nat said.

"Do you have a problem with witches?" Tom asked.

"They're everywhere," the man said. "Last night I heard them whispering outside."

I looked at Tom. The "them" was us whispering! Good thing this man hadn't caught us! We were out searching in the dark for Jim.

"But the dogs didn't bark," Nat added.

No wonder, I thought. *We were petting them*.

"Ya feeding your dog?" Tom asked.

"Of sorts," the slave said. "You want to see him?"

As we walked towards the ash hopper with Nat, I whispered to Tom, "This isn't part of the original plan."

"Plans change."

I didn't like it.

As soon as the door opened, Jim bellowed out, "Huck! And Lord, if it isn't Tom Sawyer."

"Does he know you?" Nat asked.

"What would make you think that?" Tom asked quickly.

"He called you by name."

"I didn't hear him."

"I didn't hear him," I repeated.

"Did you call our names?" Tom asked Jim.

"No," Jim said, playing along.

"It's those witches!" the slave screamed.

"You've got it awful bad," Tom said. Tom gave the poor man a dime. "You need to buy more string and tie your hair tighter."

While Tom talked with Nat, I whispered to Jim, "Don't ever let on you know us. We're going to set you free."

That night, we slid down the lightning rod. We sneaked into the lean-to next to the hut and started digging with our knives. Tom said where we dug was right behind Jim's bed. When we finally dug all the way through, no one would notice because Jim's sheets would hide the evidence. We scratched away until midnight, our hands blistered up, and we were no further along than if we'd kicked the ground with our feet.

"This isn't going to work, Huck. Hand me your knife."

He already had his knife, but I handed him mine anyway.

He threw it down!

"Hand me your *knife*. I want to be able to *say* I dug Jim out with a... *knife*."

I thought he'd lost his mind. Then I understood. I handed him a pick-axe.

I grabbed the shovel. We made good time then.

The next night, within two hours of digging, we emerged beneath Jim's bed. We crawled out, lit a candle, and awoke Jim. He called us "honey" and "child" and hugged us. He wanted us to get something to cut his ankle chain. I could see it was only looped around a leg of the bed.

"No," Tom said. "We can't rush things. Jim, be on the lookout. We'll be sending you things to help you escape on your own."

I began to wonder if I had made the right decision allowing Tom Sawyer to help me. I wanted Jim to escape. Tom wanted to make a game of it.

The next morning, Tom pushed a candle through a piece of cornbread that was going to Jim. When Nat took Jim the cornbread, we went along to see how Tom's smuggling idea would work. Jim bit down on the cornbread and nearly broke out all his teeth. (Never again did Jim eat anything without first stabbing it a few times.)

Before Jim could finish his meal, hounds started pouring out from under Jim's bed. There must have been fifteen of them. They'd smelled Jim's cornbread and come from the hole we'd dug. We'd forgotten to close the door to the lean-to on the other side.

Nat yelled "Witches!" once, keeled over on the floor, and started screaming. Tom opened the door and threw the cornbread out. The dogs followed. I ran around to the lean-to and shut the door. When we both came back, Nat was still kicking on the ground.

"What happened, Nat?" Tom asked.

"I saw witches again. They looked like the Devil's Dogs."

"You need a witch pie."

"I don't know how to make a witch pie."

"You don't?" Tom asked. "I'll make one for you."

CHAPTER FIFTEEN

Pie and Rats –
Grand Escape – Jim's Decision

Tom said he had the escape worked out, but Jim and I would have to give him time. He said if we freed Jim now, he might not get far without the whole escape route plotted out. Unfortunately, Tom was right.

Tom found a couple of nails he said a prisoner could use to write on a dungeon wall.

"Jim can't write."

"Doesn't matter," Tom said.

Tom stole some spoons and a sheet as well. He tore up the sheet and made a rope ladder with the strips. Finally, we took some flour from the house and baked the rope ladder in a pan we'd taken out of the attic. We had too much ladder for one pan. In fact, we had enough ladder for a whole meal. Tom threw the extra ladder away, took the pie to Nat, and said, "This is the witch pie. Give it to the runaway slave."

When Jim found the rope ladder in the pie, I could tell he'd thought we'd lost our minds.

Tom still hadn't told me his plan.

Tom insisted we make pens out of nails so Jim could write his name in blood. He said he had read it in books.

"You need a coat of arms," Tom said.

"I don't have a coat of any kind," Jim answered.

"You'll have one before this day is out."

While Jim and I worked making pens, Tom wrote on a piece of paper.

"I've designed your coat of arms," he said. "We'll have a bend, that's a fess, with a dog, that's a couchant, with his foot on a chain, and a motto, *Maggiore fretta, minore atto*. I got it out of a book— it means *the more haste the less speed*."

Tom might as well have spoken French. He tried to explain some things to us, but refused to explain others.

"Jim needs to write sad love poems on the wall," Tom said.

"Love poems? Jim can't write," I said.

"You can scratch them out for him. Jim can carve out what you write and then add the blood."

The next morning, we caught fifteen of the wildest rats one could ever hope for. We hid them in a cage under Aunt Sally's bed. While we looked for spiders, one of the children opened the door of the cage to see if the rats would come out. They did. We found Aunt Sally standing on the bed, screaming. The rats did their best to entertain her. We caught about a dozen more, but these weren't as lively as the first batch.

We captured spiders, bugs, frogs, and caterpillars. We tried to get a hornet's nest, but the hornets were still home. We caught a dozen garter snakes and put them in our room. I guess we didn't tie the bag tight enough, because after dinner, the bag was empty. For the next

week, snakes dropped from the ceiling and showed up in bed. At night, we could hear Aunt Sally screaming all the way to Jericho like the house was afire.

Jim did a good imitation of Aunt Sally when Tom dumped everything into Jim's hut. Jim tore the chain loose and climbed out through the hole into the lean-to. It took forever for Tom to persuade Jim to go back into the hut.

"One more day," Tom said. "A servant girl has to deliver unsigned letters to warn the family of trouble."

"What servant girl? Why do we want to warn the family? That doesn't make sense."

"That's the way the books say it's done. If you don't do this, Huck, I won't tell you the rest of the plan. Jim won't get away. Are you in?"

What choice did I have?

Tom dressed me in one of Aunt Sally's dresses and the "servant girl" wedged a message on the back door:

Beware. Trouble is brewing. Keep a sharp lookout.
        —UNKNOWN FRIEND

The next night, Tom drew a picture of a skull and crossbones and stuck it on the front door. The following night he put a picture of a coffin on the back door.

The family became all twitchy. I think they would have taken it better if the house had been full of ghosts.

Tom said it was time. Without my knowing, he wrote one final letter:

Someone is going to steal your runaway slave tonight. They've tried to scare you away, but you won't go. I'm a member of the gang, but I've suddenly got religion. I want you to catch them. When I baaa like a sheep, they'll have broken into the hut. Go in there and get them at your leisure.
                                    —UNKNOWN FRIEND

After breakfast, we sneaked over to the river, got the canoe ready, and checked the raft. When we returned, the family was all excited. They wouldn't tell us why, but Tom told me about the letter so I guessed I knew as much as they did.

That night, Tom awoke me.

"Where's the butter for the getaway lunch?"

"I put it on a piece of cornbread."

"Oh... The cornbread you forgot to pack?"

Tom took one of Aunt Sally's dresses for a disguise for Jim and climbed out the window.

He sent me downstairs to get the bread and butter. Afterwards, I was to meet him and Jim.

Aunt Sally met me at the top of the stairs as I was coming back up—so I quick hid the bread and butter under my hat. When I wouldn't tell her *why* I had been downstairs, she sent me into the living room. I wasn't alone. Fifteen farmers sat in a circle, and every one of them had a gun. I started sweating. Butter ran down my face in globs.

When Sally came into the room, one of the farmers had just said, "I'm going to get in the hut. When they come to steal the slave, I'm going to shoot them."

Aunt Sally saw the globs of melted butter running down my face and shrieked, "He's got brain fever! His brains are oozing out!"

When everyone discovered it was butter, Sally said I should have told her I was hungry. She sent me upstairs, so I climbed on down the lightning rod and met Tom and Jim, already "dressed," in the hut. I told Tom about the house full of men.

"Get ready," Tom said. "When we get a safe distance, you *baaa* like a sheep."

Suddenly we heard the tramping of feet and men's voices outside the hut.

We hit the hole and crawled into the lean-to. We heard the men bust into the hut and we all three crawled out and took off running.

"Who's that?" someone yelled.

"Answer, or we'll shoot!"

We didn't answer. Bullets started whizzing past our heads.

"They're running for the river. Unleash the dogs!"

When we heard the dogs, we jumped into the bushes. The dogs knew all three of us. We petted them. One of the hounds got the scent of a raccoon and then all the hounds took off after it. The men followed, thinking the raccoon was *us*.

When we made it safely back to the raft, I said, "Jim, you won't ever be a slave again. I promise."

Jim was happy, but I swear if I didn't think Tom was the happiest of all. His plan had worked, but more than that, *he'd been shot in the leg!* Jim tried to stop the blood with an old shirt, but it was of little use.

"We've got to get out of here," Tom said.

"Not with you bleeding like that," Jim answered. He turned to me. "Go fetch him a doctor, child."

"Jim, you're going to get caught," Tom said. "Let's go."

"My freedom isn't worth your life," Jim said.

Jim said he'd hide in the bushes when the doctor came. Then he ordered me to get help, so I hurried to bring a doctor. The last words Jim said before I left were: "After we know Tom is safe, I'll get my freedom."

CHAPTER SIXTEEN

Doctoring –
A Hero's Welcome – Freedom

I liked the doctor. He was old, nice, fatherly. "How did it happen, again?" he asked.

I retold the story. "We'd been hunting and we didn't unload our guns properly. In his sleep my brother rolled over and hit his gun. The gun went off, shooting him in the leg."

He looked at me as if he didn't quite believe me.

I thought our canoe was of good size, but the doctor said only one person could ride safely. I gave him directions and waited on the riverbank. Sometime during the night I fell asleep, for when I opened my eyes the sun had risen.

I saw no sign of the canoe. I hurried to the doctor's house and was told the doctor had been called away during the night and had not yet returned.

I started to hurry back, when a voice took me by surprise. "Where have *you* been?"

I turned, and saw Uncle Silas.

"Your aunt's been so upset for you and your brother."

"She shouldn't have been," I said. "We heard the men and the dogs last night and followed them, but they outran us. When we got to the river, we heard the dogs on the other side. We went across, got tired, and slept. Sid's at the post office."

"We'll go to the post office."

As I suspected, we didn't find Tom at the post office. Uncle Silas grew tired and took me back home with him. "Your brother will find his own way," he said.

When we arrived, neighbors crowded inside the house. A body couldn't believe the stories being told about the escaped slave.

"What creature would scribble all those sick love poems on a wall?"

"Look at that ladder of rags. He was in a

one-story hut. What did he expect to climb?"

"Those knife saws!"

"That's a week's worth for six men."

"That straw dummy he left in his own bed."

"Silas's shirt, covered in bloody writing, in an African language."

"I'd love to know what it said!"

"All those stolen items!"

"The dogs couldn't track them."

"You'd think they were a band of spirits!"

"They just disappeared!"

After everyone had gone home, Aunt Sally asked about the night before. I told her we heard the shots, slid down the lightning rod to learn of what the fuss was about, and then picked up with the same story I'd told Uncle Silas.

By supper, Tom still hadn't shown up. Uncle Silas made another trip to town. He came back alone.

Aunt Sally tucked me in bed. She hugged on me and treated me as her own child. She talked about Tom, only she called him "Sid."

"I'm going to leave the doors and windows unlocked tonight," Aunt Sally said. "I would hope you wouldn't leave and do that to me again."

I worried about Tom all night, but after what

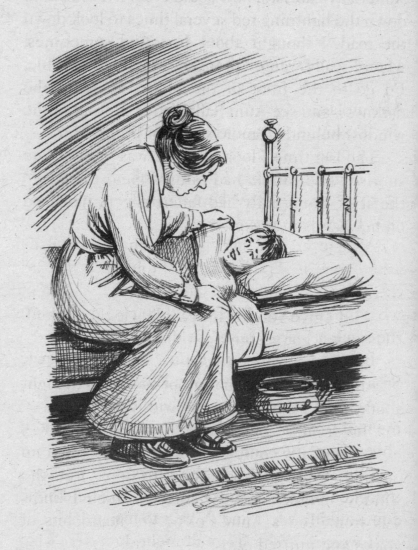

Aunt Sally had said, how could I leave? I did climb down the lightning rod several times to look down the road. I thought about Jim. And sometimes, when I really wanted to make myself feel terrible, I'd go to the front of the house, stand in the darkness, and see Aunt Sally sitting in front of the window behind a candle she kept lit for Tom.

The last time I looked at her was right before sunrise. The candle had burned almost down to the stick. Aunt Sally had fallen asleep, her head on her hands in prayer.

~ ~ ~

"Did I give you the letter?" Uncle Silas asked. "The one I got yesterday at the post office?"

"No," said Aunt Sally.

Breakfast sat cold in front of us. We all thought about Tom. I doubled my worries with Jim.

"It's from St. Petersburg. From Sis."

Before Sally could open it, a wagon pulled up outside. (When she turned to look out the window, I quick hid the letter—which I knew was from Tom's Aunt Polly.) We heard lots of voices and hurried out.

Outside stood the doctor's wagon, with Jim in the back. Jim still wore Aunt Sally's dress. Tom Sawyer lay on a mattress.

"He's dead!" Aunt Sally cried.

Tom turned his head.

"He's alive!"

They carried Tom into the house. I stayed outside, looking at Jim. I saw his eyes watering.

He didn't act like he knew me. When *my* eyes started to water, he gave me a quick glance. In my own head, I heard his voice: *You be strong, honey.* How many times had he told me that?

Some of the men wanted to hang Jim. Others said that wouldn't solve anything. The men treated Jim awful bad. Jim didn't fight back. He didn't say a word.

You be strong, honey, I thought.

They took Jim back to the hut. They put him in his clothes. They chained him with a chain around each ankle, wrist, and finally his neck. They bolted the chains to the wall.

"Feed him only bread and water," they ordered.

"If his owner doesn't come, we'll sell him at auction."

Then a voice rang out. "Don't be any rougher on him than you have to."

All eyes turned towards the doctor. He'd come from the house where he'd been tending to Tom.

"The boy went into shock right after I got there. When I mumbled aloud, 'I need somebody to help me,' this slave came out of the brush. He had no plan on running. When they tied his arms, he said only one thing—'Is that boy

going to be well?' You can't put a price on a slave like that, much less a man."

The crowd began to soften, but they still kept Jim chained and fed him nothing more.

I slept outside that night. Jim didn't want to talk. A few times I heard him cry. I lay with my head against the hut.

Next morning, I slipped into Tom's room. Aunt Sally appeared at the door and whispered, "We can all be happy now."

Tom opened his eyes. "I'm home? Where's the raft?"

"It's all right," I said.

"And Jim?"

"The same." I didn't know what else to say. Aunt Sally couldn't know that we knew Jim.

"We did it!" Tom exclaimed.

Before I could stop him, Tom went on to tell the whole story, the whole truth of it. Aunt Sally at first couldn't believe Tom's words and then her anger took over.

"And Jim's free!" Tom said.

"The runaway slave?" Aunt Sally asked. "No. He's loaded down with chains eating bread and water until he's claimed or sold."

"That isn't right!" Tom screamed. He sat up in bed. "He's a *free* man. Miss Watson died two months ago. She set him free in her Will."

"Why didn't you tell us?" Aunt Sally asked. "Why did you want to set a *free* man *free*?"

"For the adventure!" Tom said. Then he looked up and gasped, "*Aunt Polly?*"

I turned around. There stood Tom's Aunt Polly. Aunt Sally jumped for her sis. I jumped under the bed.

"Tom," said Aunt Polly, "when you get well, I'm going to beat you back to being ill. And Huck Finn, you get out from under that bed."

Aunt Polly told us that Jim was indeed free. He'd already been free *two whole months*.

I hoped that when Aunt Polly beat Tom back to being ill, she invited me to assist.

When I went outside, Jim was out of his chains and eating real food.

He walked over to me. He walked like a free man—tall, straight, proud.

"Honey, how's Tom?"

I took Jim upstairs. Tom gave Jim $40 for being such a good sport.

"This will go towards buying my family," Jim said. Hē was happy to get the money, but it didn't make me feel any better thinking about what we'd put him through.

"We can go out west," Tom said.

"Sounds fine to me," I said. "But I don't have any money. I'm sure Pap's gotten it all."

"No," Tom said. "Judge Thatcher's still holding your money."

"Your Pap isn't coming back, child," Jim said. "You remember that floating house? Remember the dead man I wouldn't let you see? That dead man was your Pap."

~ ~ ~

It's been a few weeks now. Tom's well. He wears his bullet around his neck on a string. After writing this book, I've decided I'll probably never write another one. It's too much work.

I think I'm going out west.

Aunt Sally wants to adopt me. She says she'll make me civilized.

I'd rather not.

I've been there before.

THE END

MARK TWAIN

Mark Twain's real name was Samuel Langhorne Clemens. He was born in 1835, just as Halley's Comet blazed through the sky. He grew up in Hannibal, Missouri, where he rafted on the river and had an adventurous young life.

When his father died, young Samuel went to work as a typesetter for a newspaper. He also traveled across America, working at a variety of jobs—from miner to soldier to riverboat pilot.

His own love of words and storytelling led him to become a writer. He took his pen name, Mark Twain, from a riverboat term which meant "two fathoms deep." His witty stories became very popular. In 1876, *The Adventures of Tom Sawyer* was published, which introduced America (and the world) to Tom Sawyer and Huck Finn. He published several more famous stories, such as *The Prince and the Pauper* (1882), and *A Connecticut Yankee in King Arthur's Court* (1889), but it was *The Adventures of Huckleberry Finn* (1885) which proved to be his biggest success. It is considered one of the best American novels.

Twain died in 1910, just as Halley's Comet blazed again through the sky.